CONTENTS

THREE HORSES

Movie Madness

by Cari Meister

illustrated by Heather Burns

Raintree is an imprint of Capstone Global Library Limited, a company incorporated in
England and Wales having its registered office at 264 Banbury Road, Oxford, OX2 7DY –
Registered company number: 6695582

www.raintree.co.uk
myorders@raintree.co.uk

Designed by Lori Bye
Original illustrations © Capstone Global Library Limited 2019
Originated by Capstone Global Library Ltd
Printed and bound in India

ISBN 978 1 4747 6273 1
22 21 20 19 18
10 9 8 7 6 5 4 3 2 1

British Library Cataloguing in Publication Data
A full catalogue record for this book is available from the British Library.

Acknowledgements
Design elements by Shutterstock: Semiletava Hanna

CHAPTER 1

A party plan

It was dinner time at Farley Farms. Toni, the stable manager, slipped some hay into Princess' stall.

Princess stamped her hoof and put her nose up in disgust. "Really?" she said. "Hay again? When is Toni going to take off her blinkers? I am a cat. Not a horse."

Seb, the shire horse in the next stall, smiled to himself. He looked at Princess. Her mane was plaited. Her owner, Melody, had laced a fuchsia bow into her tail. She had sparkly hoof polish on her hooves.

"I'm afraid Toni may always think you are a horse," said Seb.

"Oh pooh!" said Princess. "That's what I was afraid of!"

Princess sulked in the corner. She liked Farley Farms. Toni was a nice stable manager. She had two good horse friends. Seb and The Blizzard, an older fat little Shetland pony. Most people called The Blizzard by his stable name, Snowy. But Princess knew he preferred to be called The Blizzard, so she tried to respect that.

Princess let out a deep sigh. *If only I could get out every night, like a real cat. Then I would be really happy,* she thought.

"Cheer up," said Seb. "Did you know it's Snowy's birthday today?"

Princess' eyes opened wide. "We MUST have a party!" she said.

"A party would be fun," said Seb.
"But what about a *Tres Caballos Incognito*
birthday adventure?"

Tres Caballos Incognito means 'three
horses in disguise'. Snowy was from Mexico,
and it was the name he had given the trio
when they escaped from the stable, wearing
their fly masks as a disguise.

"Oh yes!" said Princess.

"How about going to the zoo?" asked Seb.

"What's the point in that?" said Princess.
"To stare at other animals? Boring! How
about going out for ice cream? Cats LOVE
ice cream. We could get a giant sundae and
lick it all up."

"I think Snowy is lactose intolerant," said
Seb. "Remember that time his owner gave
him some yoghurt? He groaned for three
days."

Princess frowned. "What shall we do

then?" she asked.

Seb and Princess looked out through their stall bars.

Toni was walking down the aisle, talking on her phone. "I heard that movie called *Yul the Reindeer* was really good. Where is it showing? What time? 7.00 p.m.? Perfect. See you then," she said.

Seb and Princess looked at each other. The cinema! Why didn't they think of that?

"The cinema is *purrfect!*" said Princess. "The Blizzard's always talked about going to see a movie."

CHAPTER 2

An alarm goes off

By the time Toni had switched off the lights for the night, Princess and Seb had come up with a plan.

"But how are we going to get into the cinema without being discovered?" asked Princess.

"And how are we going to get popcorn?" asked Seb. "I've always wanted to try popcorn."

Princess shrugged. "I suppose we will just have to work it out when we get there. Now use your skills and get us out of here."

"OK," said Seb. He put his lips around the latch and pulled. Soon he was standing in the aisle. A minute later, Princess was standing next to him.

They trotted down the aisle to Snowy's stall. He was asleep.

"Ahem!" said Seb. He tapped his front hoof. "OK, one, two, three."

"Happy Birthday to you! Happy Birthday to you! Happy Birthday dear THE BLIZZARD, Happy Birthday to you," they sang.

Snowy stretched and shook his mane.

"You remembered!" he said. "I thought you'd forgotten!"

"Of course not!" said Seb.

"We have a surprise birthday plan," sang Princess.

Seb wrapped his lips around Snowy's latch and slid open the furry pony's door.

Snowy trotted out.

"We need our masks," said Princess. "That way, if someone sees us, they won't know who we are."

"Great idea," said Snowy. He trotted up to the front door and grabbed a bag from his hiding place. He pulled out three fly masks.

"Where are we going?" he asked as they put on the masks.

"It's a surprise," said Princess.

"OK," said Snowy. "Do you know how to get there?"

Seb and Princess looked at each other and blinked.

"That's what I thought," said Snowy. "Let me look it up." Snowy pulled his laptop from the bag. He turned it on. Then he grabbed a hoof pick with his mouth and started pecking at the keys.

This didn't surprise Seb and Princess.

They were used to Snowy typing away. After all, he was writing a novel, *From the Horse's Mouth*.

"So where are we going?" he asked, as Seb opened the big stable door. But as he opened the door, an alarm sounded.

Tres Caballos Incognito bolted down the driveway.

The sound got quieter the further they galloped down the road.

"What was that?" asked Seb.

"I have no idea!" said Princess.

From the other direction, they heard another siren – NEE-NAW, NEE-NAW. A police car was buzzing down the road towards Farley Farms.

AAWWWW! The horses stood in the middle of the road, snorting. They looked in all directions.

"Let's hide in the trees," said Princess.

"Good idea," said Snowy. "The noises can't get us there."

CHAPTER 3

Princess disappears

Tres Caballos Incognito hid in the trees.
Soon the noises stopped.

"What a crazy night!" said Seb.

"I wonder what is going on," said Snowy.

Seb shrugged.

"So where are we going?" asked Snowy.

Seb opened his mouth into a big, toothy
grin. "The cinema!" he said.

"The cinema?" said Snowy. "How
wonderful! I've always wanted to go to the
cinema. What movie are we going to see?"

"*Yul the Reindeer,*" said Seb.

Snowy pulled out his laptop and typed:
YUL THE REINDEER.

He read, "*Yul the Reindeer* is sure to delight even the most finicky movie critic. It has it all – adventure, beautiful scenery, cute animals and romance." Snowy looked up.

"It sounds great!" said Princess. "It has all the elements I love in books."

Seb looked confused. "What does *finicky* mean?"

Snowy typed it into his laptop. He cleared his throat. "*The Horse's Dictionary* writes: *finicky means picky, fussy or critical.*"

Seb rolled his eyes. "I totally get it," he said.

"Princess, does that make sense to you?" asked Snowy.

But Princess wasn't there.

"Princess! Where are you?" called Snowy.

Princess didn't answer.

Seb was annoyed. "How could she just disappear like that?" he asked. "We might be late for the movie!"

Snowy whinnied into the dark. "Princess!"

Princess did not whinny back.

CHAPTER 4

A rabbit

Princess was busy chasing a rabbit across the field.

Finally, she thought. *Some real feline action.*

The rabbit was fast.

But Princess was fast too. She gritted her teeth and ran like the wind.

The rabbit stopped for a second to look back. He wondered what on earth a horse was doing chasing him. Surely, she was not going to eat him. So he stopped.

Princess stopped too.

Why is he stopping? she wondered. *This was just getting fun! Doesn't he know that all the fun is in the chase? Now I have to just eat him.*

Princess bent her long head down next to the rabbit. She sniffed. Then . . . AAAACHOOO! She sneezed.

ACHOO!

She sniffed again.

AAAACHOO!

Her sneeze was so loud that Seb and Snowy heard her.

They came galloping over.

"What are you doing over here?" asked Seb. "We are going to be late for the movie!"

But Princess was slumped over. She was crying.

"I can't believe it!" she said. "I finally caught a rabbit."

"Well, that's good news, isn't it?" asked Snowy.

"Yes. But I can't eat it," cried Princess.

"Well," said Seb, "horses are not supposed–"

"What happened?" asked Snowy, nudging Seb for his slip-up.

"Didn't you hear me sneeze?" said Princess. "I must be allergic to rabbits!"

Seb wanted to feel sorry for her, but he couldn't. He wanted to get to the movie. "I bet you aren't allergic to popcorn," he said. "Let's get going!"

Snowy patted Princess on the shoulder. "It's always hard when you find out things you'd rather not know. But try to look on the bright side. We are going to the cinema!"

CHAPTER 5

A box

By the time Snowy had worked out the best route to the cinema, Princess had got over her sadness.

"Oooh! I can't wait," she said. They trotted through the back alleys to get to the cinema.

"Let's hide behind those rubbish bins," said Snowy. "We don't want to be seen."

"How are we going to get into the cinema?" asked Princess. "It's not like we can walk in the front door."

"Wait here," said Snowy. "I will check it out. Don't worry. I will stick to the shadows."

Seb grabbed a large box from the bins. "Put this on," he said.

"How will I see?" asked Snowy.

"Give me your hoof pick," said Seb.

Snowy handed Seb the pick.

"There," said Seb as he poked three holes in the box.

Seb placed the box over Snowy.

"How do I look?" Snowy asked.

"You look like a box," said Princess.

"Well, it must be working then," said Snowy.

Snowy slowly walked towards the back door of the cinema. Just as he got within two strides, the door creaked opened.

CHAPTER 6

Statues

A man from the cinema stared at the big box in front of him. Snowy froze.

The man scratched his head. "That's strange. I thought I put that box in the bins," he said. The man was carrying a big bin bag. He tapped the top of the box. "I'll be back for you," he said to the box.

It was a loud, scary sound. Snowy did everything he could to stop himself getting scared. If he got scared, he would do a poo. The man would find the horses, and the birthday adventure would be over.

The man left the box and started walking towards the bins.

"Oh no!" said Snowy.

But Princess and Seb were one step ahead.

Seb found a trolley behind the bins. He pushed it in the opposite direction. It rolled and crashed in the far alley.

"What is going on around here?" said the cinema man. As he walked over to the alley, *Tres Caballos Incognito* scrambled around the corner. They sneaked through the back door of the cinema.

Seb closed the door. "You can only open it from the inside," he said, smiling. "That man will have to go to the front to get back in. That will give us more time to find where to go."

"Good thinking," said Snowy.

The three friends poked their heads into the foyer. The movie was about to start, so there were a few people around.

Seb stuck his nose in the air and inhaled. "I smell popcorn!" he said.

Just then, a small boy turned around. His eyes went big. He tugged on his mother's sleeve. "Mummy! Mummy!" he said. "This cinema has real horses!"

Seb, Snowy and Princess froze.

The mother was too busy chatting with another woman to turn around. "That's nice, dear," she said without looking.

"Mummy, Mummy!" said the boy. "Look!"

"Stay very, very still," said Snowy. "Pretend you are a statue."

The boy's mother finally turned around. She squinted. "Those are just cardboard horses," she said. "They make them look so real."

The boy didn't believe her. His mother took him by the hand and led him away.

"Phew!" said Seb.

"That was close!" said Princess.

"The movie is almost starting," said Snowy. "I bet we can sneak in now."

Somehow they did.

CHAPTER 7

Yul the Reindeer

It was Tuesday. There were only a handful of people in the cinema. *Tres Caballos Incognito* found a wide row of seats at the back. The movie was just starting. No one seemed to notice them.

"We didn't get any popcorn!" said Seb.

"Maybe when the movie is over, we will find a half-eaten bag," said Snowy.

Seb hoped that would be true.

The music got louder as Yul the reindeer made his first appearance on the big screen. He was majestic!

"Wow," whispered Princess. "If I was a hooved mammal, I might love him."

The three friends watched as Yul met a beautiful reindeer called Holly. They were perfect together. But one day, Holly got lost in a blizzard.

"Go and find her," Seb whispered to the screen. "You must find your true love!"

Yul seemed to listen. He crunched through the blizzard searching for Holly. Soon he came to a big lake.

"The ice is too thin," whispered Snowy. "Go back through the woods instead."

Unfortunately, Yul did not listen to Snowy's advice.

Yul slowly stepped onto the thin ice. The music rose.

"I can't watch!" said Princess. She buried her head under her leg, but peeked through just enough so she could still see.

The ice began to *crack, crack, crack* . . . and then it broke. Yul splashed into the icy waters. He scrambled to get back up on the ice, but he couldn't get a grip. It was too slippery. Then all of a sudden there was a ROAR!

Yul turned around. It was a grizzly bear!

The audience screamed. Princess hid her face. And Seb? He just couldn't help it. He was so scared, he dropped a large pile of steaming poo.

Snowy noticed right away.

"Seb!" said Snowy.

"I'm so sorry!" Seb said. "I couldn't help it!"

The audience noticed too.

"What is that smell?" someone yelled in the dark.

The cinema man came in with a torch.

Tres Caballos Incognito tried to hide. But there was nowhere to go.

The torch beam revealed the horses in all their glory.

The cinema man jumped back.

"Stop the movie," he shouted. "Turn on the lights!"

"Nothing to do now, but just own up," said Snowy. "Look like the noble steeds we are. Perhaps they won't get too angry."

"No chance I'm going to get any popcorn now," Seb said.

The big lights clicked on.

CHAPTER 8

New friends

The audience gasped. One big man at the front laughed.

The boy smiled. "See mummy!" he said. "I told you there were horses in here."

Just then, a familiar voice was heard. "What on earth?"

It was Toni. She was at the movie too. She walked up to the horses. "Snowy? Princess? Seb?" she asked.

The cinema man glared at her. "Do you know these horses?" he asked. "Did you bring them here? What were you thinking?"

Toni stumbled a bit. "Yes, I know them. No, I didn't bring them here. I am not sure how they escaped. I just put in a new alarm system. If they got out, I should have been notified."

Princess rubbed her head against Toni. She was glad Toni was here.

Toni pulled her phone from her pocket. The screen was black.

"I forgot that I turned my phone off for the movie," she said.

Toni turned her phone back on. There were five alerts flashing.

YOU HAVE 5 NOTIFICATIONS:

! ALERT !

! ALERT !

! ALERT !

! ALERT !

! ALERT !

"I am so sorry," said Toni. "I will get them out of here straight away." She picked up her handbag and popcorn.

Seb saw his chance. He nudged his way closer and grabbed the bag.

The audience laughed.

"Looks like he wants some popcorn," said the big man at the front.

The little boy ran up. "Are they friendly?" he asked.

"Yes," said Toni.

The people came closer. "Look at the little white one. He is so cute! Can we stroke him?"

Toni nodded. "Of course," she said. "He likes the attention."

It was true. Snowy loved it.

Everyone oohed and ahhed. They asked Toni questions as they stroked and fed the horses popcorn.

"And that big one – is he a shire horse?"

"Do you think they liked the movie?"

"Are reindeer related to horses?" asked another.

Next, they all wanted selfies with the horses. Then they wanted to watch the movie. They convinced the cinema man to start it again.

"Well, OK," he said, looking at Toni. "But can you clean that up first?" The man nodded towards Seb's pile.

"Of course," said Toni. "I will just run out to my truck and grab a shovel."

CHAPTER 9

Happily ever after

By the time the three friends were back in their stalls, they were tired but happy.

"That was the best birthday ever," said Snowy. "Thank you."

"It was a great movie," said Seb. "I can't believe Yul was able to fight off the bear."

"Yes, but not before losing a leg!" said Princess. "I can't believe he hopped all that way to rescue Holly."

"Then they lived happily ever after," said Snowy.

"Yes," said Princess. "Happily ever after."

Snowy pulled out his laptop. He typed for
a little while.

"What are you writing?" asked Seb.

"I've just finished adding a famous quote to my novel. I was reminded of it tonight at the cinema. It is from the ancient Greek philosopher Xenophon."

"What did he say?" yawned Princess.

Snowy cleared his throat. He read:

"And indeed, a horse who bears himself proudly is a thing of such beauty and astonishment that he attracts the eyes of all beholders.

No one will tire of looking at him as long as he will display himself in all his splendour."

"People love us don't they?" asked Seb.

"Yes, they do," said Snowy. "But they should. We are noble creatures. There is not another animal as glorious as the horse."

"I'm glad you are my friend," said Seb. "You help me see things."

"I'm glad you are my friend too," said Snowy. "Besides, we'd never get out of here for adventures if it wasn't for you. Isn't that true, Princess?"

But Princess was already asleep, dreaming of an adventure yet to come.

GLOSSARY

advice suggestions about what to do about a problem

allergic when something, such as a bee sting or pollen in the air, makes someone feel unwell; many allergies make you sneeze

critic person who points out the good and bad in something

disguise something that hides you by making you look like something else

disgust strong feeling of dislike

feline any animal of the cat family

fly mask mask used to protect a horse's eyes and jaw from flies

glorious wonderful, beautiful

lactose intolerant when someone's body is not able to process a certain type of sugar found in milk and dairy products

mammal warm-blooded animal that breathes air; mammals have hair or fur

noble something or someone that is of high rank in society

philosopher person who studies truth and knowledge

respect believe in the quality and worth of others and yourself

route road or course followed to get somewhere

steed horse, especially one that is lively

sulk be angry and silent

ABOUT THE AUTHOR

Cari Meister has written more than 130 books for children, including the Tiny series (Penguin) and the Fast Forward Fairy Tales series (Scholastic). Cari is a school librarian and she loves to visit other schools and libraries to talk about the joy of reading and writing. Cari lives in the mountains of Colorado, USA, with her husband, four boys, one horse and one dog.

ABOUT THE ILLUSTRATOR

Heather Burns is an illustrator from Uttoxeter, UK. In 2013, she graduated from the University of Lincoln with a degree in illustration and has been working as a freelance illustrator ever since. Heather has a passion for bringing stories to life with pictures and hopes that her work makes people smile. When she's not working she's usually out walking her grumpy black Labrador, Meadow!

TALK ABOUT IT

1. Are *Tres Caballos Incognito* good friends? Give three examples from the story to support your answer.

2. Seb and Snowy never try to convince Princess that she's a horse. Why do you think that is?

3. Was the audience's reaction to *Tres Caballos Incognito* surprising to you? Why or why not?

WRITE ABOUT IT

1. Write a different ending! What would've happened if Toni hadn't been in the cinema?

2. Write a chapter of Snowy's novel *From the Horse's Mouth*.

3. Write the last chapter from the cinema man's point of view. What does he think about the horses being in the cinema?

BOOKS IN THE
THREE HORSES SERIES

Clever Fields Fiasco

Movie Madness

Roller Coaster Ride

Seaside Escape

THE FUN
DOESN'T STOP HERE!

Discover more at
www.raintree.co.uk